Book cover illustrated by Brian Urrutia.

Note for Librarians: A cataloguing record for this book is available from Library and Archives Canada at www.collectionscanada.ca/amicus/index-e.html
ISBN 1-4251-0578-5

Offices in Canada, USA, Ireland and UK

Book sales for North America and international:
Trafford Publishing, 6E–2333 Government St.,
Victoria, BC V8T 4P4 CANADA
phone 250 383 6864 (toll-free 1 888 232 4444)
fax 250 383 6804; email to orders@trafford.com
Book sales in Europe:
Trafford Publishing (UK) Limited, 9 Park End Street, 2nd Floor
Oxford, UK OX1 1HH UNITED KINGDOM
phone +44 (0)1865 722 113 (local rate 0845 230 9601)
facsimile +44 (0)1865 722 868; info.uk@trafford.com
Order online at:
trafford.com/06-2336

10 9 8 7 6 5 4 3 2

To my son
Brian
whose spirit
has lit my path
making the dark days
light and full of love

PAST
BECOMES PRESENT

By

Rebecca T. Urrutia

CHAPTER ONE

It was a day like none Dave could remember before. The thunderous purple clouds moved rapidly; haunting drumming echoed through the canyons; the winds screamed as they whipped around him and the vivid red rocks of Sedona filled him with visions of faceless Indian squaws. In that moment his life changed forever.

Over and over again these visions appeared to him. He was so overwhelmed that he was compelled to paint them with a ferocity that left him without sleep for days.

As the days progressed he tried to analyze the fury that had overcome him, extracting meaning from all that occurred. It was as if the spirits were telling him something.

But what?

He was reading an article on hiking in Northern Arizona and came across pictures of the cliff dwellings at Palatki. That was when the visions started. He visualized climatic changes not corresponding with the seasons -- white buffalo, wolves, birds -- all migrating at a rapid pace. Tribesmen searched for food and no animals were in sight while the squaws who emanated mysterious colors through- out their bodies washed clothes at a stream and carried water uphill to their dwellings. Crops had not produced and the people danced savagely around the fire pits chanting to the Kachina spirits for rain.

Later came a vision of an assault on the village but only fragments were presented. All this bothered him deeply. Why was he chosen to see what no one else could? Were the souls trying to tell their stories? What could he possibly do?

Weeks passed when his agent called him.

"Dave, I would like to see what you've created lately."

"Well, you'll not believe your eyes," he responded.

"Why? What is it?" Jeff asked

"I have never painted anything like this," he said.

"When can I take a look?"

"How about tomorrow at 3 p.m.?" he replied.

"See you then."

"Magnificent! Where did you come up with the color schemes?" Jeff asked.

"I don't know how. They just came to me," he responded.

" Do you know what you have done?" replied Jeff.

"No, what?"

"Not only have you created hues not used before but you have visualized another theory. It was unknown why these people mysteriously vanished, their disappearance remains a mystery. Now, we can conceive that the assault was the reason for their evanescence. A celebration is in order. All this will make an exciting exhibition. How about it?" Jeff asked.

"Fine," he replied.

"These are worth more than the last ones," Jeff replied.

"Yes, I will never forget the amount received for them."

"Your talent is incredible, Dave, your technique, brush strokes; the colors are so vibrant they come alive. So much excitement is exhibited here. No one has been able to capture that since the great masters. After all, art history is my expertise, and you can also thank my father and grandfather for teaching me all they knew in establishing the value in art and dealing with clients."

"Being brought up as a museum curator has suited you well," Dave commented.

His mother was charming, elegant and stupendous in entertaining. It was no wonder they as a team were greeted graciously by the elite society.

Jeff stood six feet tall, black hair, clear green eyes perfectly groomed. He was born into a life of luxury that of which only a privileged few attain. The best cars, yachts and the women flocked over him. At an early age he was fascinated with art and sculpture and he enjoyed helping his father at the museum. He had impeccable taste; he knew what and when to sell and his energetic personality, along with a magnetic smile, grabbed everyone he met. He had the world at his fingertips.

Weeks passed and Dave desperately needed rest and relaxation. Getting away from everyone seemed like the perfect idea and he drove along the coastline. Getting out of his car to get a better view of the cliffs, rocks and ocean, he followed a trail which guided him up the bluff to an animal park. He wandered around, yet something kept pulling him to the west and visions of the faceless Indian squaws began appearing to him. He thought he would never get away from the spirits who had taken over his life. All he wanted was tranquility.

Then he saw her. It was a bright sunny day; her long, blonde, wavy hair blew with the ocean breezes as it whipped around her face. Her velvety golden tan skin and turquoise eyes sparkled with radiance. Her tall, slender, provocative body walked along the bluffs and the scent of jasmine filled the air.

Desiree found it delightful feeding the lorikeets as they fluttered around her. Then, they flew over to the stranger at the corner of the gate. Their eyes met. They smiled, and could not take their eyes off each other. Her heart pounded. She could not contain her excitement. It was as if she had been waiting a lifetime for this moment. The lorikeets then flew back to her and he came walking confidently towards her. He stood there tall, bronze and rugged-looking; his salt and pepper hair, sapphire-blue eyes and chiseled body set her heart on fire.

"I guess they are trying to tell us something. My name is Dave."

"I believe they are. My name is Desiree."

His smile was warm, tender and he had the most irresistible dimple.

The lorikeets fluttered freely around both of them. Cupid's arrow had just penetrated.

They were so drawn to each other that they lost track of the time. "We are closing now. Please exit by the far gate," the keeper said, interrupting them.

Dave walked her to her car and they stood there watching the palm trees blow gently and the waves crashing against the rocks. The seagulls screeched as they flew against the most incredible colors as they embraced the sky. Paradise had just arrived.

"Is this your favorite place?" he asked.

"Yes, it is, but I hadn't planned on being here today." She looked confused.

"Then, why are you here?"

"You may think it strange, but I was drawn here today. I just felt I needed to be here," she responded.

"I am happy you did." He smiled enthusiastically. "I had the same urge."

"Do you believe in destiny?" she asked.

"Well, I hadn't until now." He smiled warmly. "May I see you again?" he asked.

"I would like that very much," she replied.

Weeks passed and she didn't heard from him. She was beginning to think he wasn't interested. Then the phone rang.

"Hi, this is Dave. How are you?"

Her heart raced. She was excited but tried not to show her eagerness. "I am just fine, thank you," she replied.

He elaborated on a deadline he had been working on.

"What do you do?" she asked.

"I am an artist," he replied.

"What is it you paint?" she asked.

"I paint images that come to me; the feelings are so vivid that I am compelled to paint them. Many are mystic, while others depict the culture of the Sinagua Indians. I believe I am being called," he said.

"Who is calling you?" she asked innocently.

"When I close my eyes I am surrounded by magnificent red rocks and I hear drumming as the winds roar. It is a feeling so intense that nothing stops me from painting it. When this urgency comes it is a calling. The spirits are urging me to fulfill something," he said.

"Why are they calling you?" she asked.

" I am not sure but I feel connected. It's hard to describe."

"I would be interested in seeing your work, if you will let me," she said.

"Sure, how about tomorrow?" he replied.

"Great, what time shall I be at your studio?"

"Anytime after 2 p.m.," he said.

The next day she arrived to see him still working on his creations. He stopped to show her and explain how the visions came to be. His studio was filled with the spirit of the wilderness, encompassed with paintings that showed the history of the Sinaguas, from sunrises, sunsets, thunderstorms, lightning, and spirit communication, to their daily lives, along with the incredible views of the cliff dwellings.

When he showed her the painting of the attack on the camp, fear overwhelmed her and her legs grew weak and she grasped for air.

"I don't want to die," she cried out.

"Desiree, you're okay. You're not going to die. Everything is all right." He looked at her stunned. "Just what did you see to make you react that way?"

"For some odd reason I thought it was me," she explained, still out of breath.

"That's impossible. You are here safe with me." He hugged her gently. "Come on, let's go out and get some sunshine."

It was a beautiful sunny day and they walked along the ocean. She was enchanted by watching the children build sand castles and digging up shells. The salt air and ocean breezes comforted her; color was coming back into her face.

"Are you feeling better?" he asked.

"Little bit," she replied. "It's about time for me to be heading back."

"Would you like me to drive you home?" he asked.

"I'll be okay," she replied.

The next day he called to see how she was doing.

"I am doing great. What's happening with you?" she asked.

"Well, I'm happy to hear you so cheerful," he said. "I am sorry that your visit to my studio was so disturbing," he replied.

"Dave, don't worry. I am over it now," she said.

"That's great. Would you be interested in spending the day at sea? We can charter a yacht and enjoy the fresh air," he offered.

"Wonderful. I would like that very much," she replied.

"How does tomorrow sound?" he said.

" Okay," she replied.

"Fine. What time and where do I pick you up?" he asked.

"My address is 1517 Ocean Blvd. Pick me up at nine in the morning," she replied.

It was a perfect morning and they boarded the yacht. Most of the morning they spent laying on the deck sunbathing, watching the water glistening, waves swelling the salt air and the wind in their hair were all invigorating.

Lunch soon arrived and the crew had prepared a fish sampler dish, pilaf, assorted salad greens and a peach cobbler for dessert. Every beverage was available to them but champagne seemed to be the best choice. The table dressed with white linens, fine silver, yellow roses embraced with white baby breaths and ice sculpture was an incredible sight.

"You're just beautiful, Desiree." He softly looked into her eyes, then kissed her and held her tightly in his arms.

She looked into his eyes, her eyes sparkling with love, then kissed him back. "Yes, this is a wonderful day."

They walked to the front of the yacht. Desiree tossed her head from side to side, enjoying the salt air filtering through her hair and the ocean breezes against her face. She smiled then gave Dave a peck on the cheek.

"Do you like exploring? Is this something you do often?" she asked.

"I am like a child when I get the chance to explore. I enjoy traveling and watching animals of all kinds in their natural habitat. The most disturbing was when I was in Africa. I saw poachers slaughtering animals for monetary gain, making many endangered species. That was when I became active in their support."

"I noticed your eyes gleaming with excitement. It is wonderful to see you come alive like this." She smiled warmly.

"I've participated in volunteer programs for abused children for many years. It just broke my heart to see them battered and I wanted to make a difference. They deserve healthier lives and chance to become all they can be. Their openness and unsuspecting nature is something I wish everyone could hang on to forever and their pure laughter brings much joy. I support all programs available to them," Desiree said.

"I knew you loved children, by the way you watched them build sand castles. I could see the happiness it brought to you. You're a warm and nurturing person. I love that about you," Dave said.

As they glazed over the side of the yacht a school of dolphins leaped in the air. They smiled at each other as the babies scurried next to their mothers. Soon the pod was out of sight. Then pelicans flew above them diving for food in the sparkling water. Oh, how she wished the day would not end. The sun was starting to set with it the most amazing colors of purples, oranges and yellows against the sky. They clung and kissed passionately.

It would take two long hours to get back and the crew hustled around preparing a table filled with fresh fruit and assorted cheese for snacking. She was sad to see the marvelous day end and as she glanced at Dave, it was obvious that he felt the same. They packed up as they arrived at the port and he drove her home.

"Dave, this day was incredible. I will keep it in my heart forever," she said.

"Yes, I had a wonderful time too," he said, smiling, his eyes full of love. Then he planted a kiss on her cheek. "I am planning on taking a trip soon," he said. "Would you like to go with me?"

"Yes. Sounds exciting," she replied. "Where are we going?"

"Sedona, Arizona, is where the tribe originated," he answered. "But before that, how about dinner Wednesday evening?"

"That would be wonderful. You can pick me up at 6:oo p.m."

Minutes before Dave was due to arrive Desiree could not decide what to wear. Like a tornado whipping through her closet, clothes lay everywhere; she wanted to look her best because he thrilled her so. She didn't want him to ever leave her sight. That was how she became around him. She was clinging desperately.

"You look stunning," Dave remarked and planted a kiss on her cheek. He just couldn't take his eyes off of her.

"Thank you," she said, while her eyes glimmered.

They had dinner at a lovely place along the ocean. Candles were lit, fresh flowers brightened their table, and the sounds of Rachmaninoff's Rhapsody made their evening perfect.

"What was your childhood like?" she asked, sipping on a glass of champagne.

"My parents were poor immigrants. I wore hand-me-downs and they never fit right. The children at school made fun of my clothing and from there on, I swore I would make something of myself. I worked my way through college. My art instructors were excited about my work and introduced me to influential people, who helped me obtain scholarships. I could have never done it without them. In the ensuing years, out of gratitude, I paid them back more then they had funded me. They wanted nothing in return but I insisted," he said.

"Well, you sure did. Look at you now." She smiled and blushed. "My mother raised me alone; we went everywhere together. Our relationship was one of sisters instead of that of mother-daughter. We lived in the country and I enjoyed picking and smelling wildflowers, watching the squirrels as they got on their hind legs to eat. Their twitching nose and curious eyes was the most precious sight. I even tried talking to them, you know."

"Well, did they answer you?" He smiled with the largest grin she had ever seen.

" I imagined they did. Isn't it funny how children entertain themselves?" she replied.

" I guess I can say I had my moments also," he said. "Now that we have a little history on each other and I know that the squirrel is not going to cut in, let's dance?" he asked.

" I'd love to." She radiated with a glow.

The sun was setting as they danced along the patio.

"You're so beautiful." He brushed his hands along her face. Soon his lips engulfed hers.

"Well, now I see how you've been spending your nights," a woman yelled.

"What is the matter with you? You don't own me," he said to the intruder.

"What's going on here? I want an explanation," remarked Desiree.

"Sherry is my business partner and I will make sure she doesn't ever do this again. Now, let's get out of here," he said.

As they left the restaurant he put his arms tightly around Desiree. She knew at that moment that this was the man with whom she would spend eternity. She had a compelling feeling that she had known him before. They walked along the oceanside talking and kissing: neither of them wanting to let go.

The next day she found herself rushing around, getting ready for her appointments. She loved working out of her home; she had lived there for seven years and had it specially built. The entry way had skylights and a large ancient table filled with fresh arrangements of flowers. It was cheerful and bright.

The rest of the home was spacious. Soft neutral colors was the theme, stoned pathways, terra cotta floors, Venetian marble counter tops, delicately carved furniture gave it an exotic look and plants enhanced every niche. Light glimmered in all the rooms and looking out of the windows at the manicured landscape and endless rows of flowers was delightful. She enjoyed breakfast on the patio where she could watch the birds fluttering in the bird bath.

As a designer, it gave her the opportunity to meet new people and create an exciting home for them. As a child she had sat at her desk many hours drawing the interior of houses. She enjoyed arranging different rooms and working with many colors. She never dreamed that she would one day be a well- known designer. Now her favorite activity was waking up early to a beautiful sunrise and watching the sun set. It provided such a spiritual uplift that her heart sang with joy.

It had been a long day; she had had several productive meetings with clients. Evening came and the phone rang.

"Hi, honey, how was your day?" Dave asked.

"Went great," she replied. "How was yours?"

"Fine, fine. Everything is smoothing out now," he remarked. "I would like to invite you over to see my home. How about it?"

"I would love to," she replied.

"Fine. I will pick you up tomorrow at six," he said.

As they entered Desiree's eyes lit up. It was immaculate. He led her outdoors overlooking the most dramatic coastline she had ever seen. They walked down a private trail which meandered into a secluded cove. There were more stars than they had ever seen and they both marveled as they twinkled brightly. With waves rushing up the shoreline unveiling the deep mystery of the sea, she looked into his eyes. He held her tightly in his arms and kissed her savagely. His tongue hot and wet roaming down her neck to her breasts, she pulled him closer. He cradled her buttocks and pushed her into him. He slid his hands to her bottom parts.

"Oh, darling, please stop," she pleaded.

"Don't you want me?" he asked.

"Yes, but I need more time."

"If you really want me to," he replied.

"Yes, I do," she said, panting for breath.

"Let's head up to the house."

The stoned pathway was marvelously designed as if she had just entered a European chateau. Soon they were in the living room where sculpture, flowers and plants enhanced the area. Lavish tapestries adorned the walls, velvet sofa sectionals and recliners filled the room with comfort and elegance. They talked and laughed. He was funny, witty and charming.

"Let me show you the rest of the house before dinner," he said.

Soon they were going upstairs.

"Let's start with this one," he said.

It was representing the Roman Empire. The walls all hand painted displaying the era's daily life, the pleasure they embraced and massive columns depicting their stupendous architecture. The bedroom furniture had been acquired at museum auctions. She immediately felt she had just walked into the past.

"Did you do the paintings on the walls?" she asked.

"Yes, I did," he responded.

Next they walked into the Egyptian room, where the granite blocks enveloped the pyramid, vivid colors liberated the walls and statues. The furnishing of that era was most impressive. She could imagine Cleopatra lounging and being pampered by her servants.

"This one is my favorite," he said.

She entered the African safari room, where the terrain and endangered species covered the walls. As she looked into their eyes, it was as if those majestic beasts cried out in sadness and despair. She wept as these feelings overwhelmed her. Its furnishing were of rattan and palms. It was an amazing depiction.

Tahiti was the theme of the next room. Entering, she was soothed by its pristine waters and the most spectacular shades of purple, pink and orange depicting a sunset. Thatch-roof huts dotted the coast, the rush of the tide and foamy white bubbles raced to the shore almost seemed to echo in that room, enveloped by a canopy bed covered with palm leaves. It was a haven that was difficult to leave.

The Grand Canyon was next, an amphitheatre fit for the gods, encompassed by its prismatic colors surfacing the horizon highlighting the awesome view of bald eagles soaring over canyons. Mule trails leading to the bottom were displayed by panoramic views at each turn. The incredible natural beauty was mesmerizing. The room was set up in a camping atmosphere. Lantern style lamps hung and camping gear lay around the tent.

The next two bedrooms were more traditional and comfortable, for guests who did not want a cultural experience. All rooms had large scenic windows, so the ocean was the focal point.

"Which one do you sleep in?" she asked.

"I try a different one each night; I like the inspiration," he responded.

"This place is a museum in its own. What inspired you to do this?" she asked.

" I have to be consistently stimulated and this keeps my creativity flowing," he explained.

"I make the best sautéed shrimp. It's time for dinner."

"Sounds great," she said.

She helped him. He prepared the shrimp; she did the salad, set the table and lit the candles. It smelled marvelous. They both sat and talked as they ate.

"Gee, I didn't know you were a chef too. This is great," she proclaimed.

"Why thank you. I am happy you enjoyed it," he replied.

" I had a marvelous evening. It's getting late. Can you take me home?" she asked.

"Of course," he replied.

It was an hour drive and soon they were at her door where he planted a gentle kiss on her cheek.

"I am ready to go to Sedona. When can you go?"

"I need to finish the job that I am working on. How about two weeks time?"

"Great, I'll make all the arrangements," he said.

The next day Desiree had lunch with a client. They were discussing what materials to use for drapes. Suddenly, Sherry joined their table.

"I need to speak with you, Desiree," she insisted.

"Please excuse me," Desiree said to her client. She motioned for Sherry to follow. "Just what is it you want?"

"I want to give you advice. Don't fall head over heels for Dave. He'll dump you in no time. You don't have what he wants and you never will. He likes the chase, but after you have been captured, it's the end."

"What do you mean?" she asked.

"He's promiscuous and you don't have enough money." Sherry smirked.

She walked back to her client, but found it hard to focus as they continued to finalized their plans.

"Dave, is that you?" Desiree asked that evening.

"Yes, what's up?" he replied.

" Sherry interrupted a meeting I was having today. I want to know just what she is to you. She's disrupting my life and I just don't feel good about it."

"Well, what happened?" he asked.

She told him what the woman had said.

"Sherry is a rich snob and she is used to getting what she wants at all costs. From the beginning I told her I had no interest in her personally, that our relationship was strictly business. She won't let go and now it is getting out of hand. I told her I was going to see an attorney to cancel our business agreement. I didn't think she would do anything. Can't you see she was just trying to get you upset? She knows that I love you dearly. Please don't let her get to you," he replied.

"Okay, darling, you are probably right."

She didn't want to lose Dave and Sherry was so envious of their love, she figured the woman would do anything to discourage her. So she had to brush that out of her mind and not let anything break up their relationship.

She would be thankful when the arrangement was cancelled and Sherry would be out of Dave's life for good. She just hoped it wouldn't take too long.

CHAPTER TWO

Spring was upon them; Dave stood at Desiree's door. The sun had not come up yet, but the morning air was brisk and refreshing. The smell of pine filtered through the air and he was filled with exuberance and excitement as they packed the car and headed for Sedona.

He preferred driving so they could stop and explore the surroundings. The sun was now coming up; warm yellows against the blue sky hinted at beautiful day.

Their first stop was a café adjoining an Indian Trading Post. The aroma of fresh coffee filled the air. As they entered, Hopi Indians were talking and laughing. Dave had the strangest feeling, as they passed them and found intensity in their eyes as they watched him. They had finished breakfast and had to walk past the Indian to get to the gift shop. When they did the Indians looked at Dave.

"See you again, Hotevilla."

Dave looked at Desiree confused. She smiled and shrugged.

Then they browsed through the shop. Navajo rugs hung on the walls, Kachina dolls and jewelry filled the displays while incense penetrated the air. She was drawn to a beautiful antique turquoise necklace with intricate designs. Her eyes sparkled as she admired it and she lingered at the display.

"Do you like it?" he asked.

"It's a little expensive," she replied.

"The love we share means more to me than anything on this earth," he said. "It's yours." He paid for it, and then placed it around her neck. "You're absolutely beautiful." His lips met hers.

Desiree now felt she belonged to Dave totally. She had never believed in that type of relationship before, but she loved him so much that she was willing to consider it.

Upon arriving in Sedona, Micki greeted them as they walked into the lobby of the rental office. Her hair was golden red. She had high cheekbones and the warmest brown eyes. She wore a pastel pink blouse, a mystical heart necklace, navy jeans and walked with a childish wiggle as she led them to their cabin. She chattered endlessly and Desiree worried they would never get to close the door.

The cabin was built of cobblestone and ivy enveloped the entrance. Once inside, she found the fireplace warm and cozy. The mantel was adorned with an assortment of pink and yellow roses and magnificent silver candleholders. When they opened the windows they had a spectacular view of the red rocks. The babble of the creek nearby was soothing.

She rushed to her suitcase to take out the scented candles she had brought. She lit the wicks, turned on music and poured champagne. They drank and drank. As they danced their bodies met and they were heated with passion. They stumbled to the bed engulfed in each other's arms.

He slid his hands slowly up her thighs. Then wrapped his legs around her, kissing her passionately, then he thrust himself inside her. Engulfed in his fire, she soared to heights she had not been before, all the while moaning with pleasure. He turned on his side as he slept and she smiled at the love swelling inside her.

Morning came and she was still filled with passion. She climbed over him kissing and fondling him. He pulled her into him eagerly. They continued thrusting upon each other till they both reached ecstasy together. She had never been happier in all her life.

"Desiree, you're not like any of the women I have known. It's refreshing. You're fun loving, light-hearted, warm and your inner spiritually takes my breath away. I don't know how I ever made it without you," he whispered.

She hugged, kissed and gave him her enchanting smile.

The vivid colors of the red rock gave them so much energy. They spent the early hours having coffee and peach filled croissants by the stream at Cathedral Rock, which gently drew them into its peace. The rustling wind and morning sun filtered through the trees. The rippling water and delicate sounds of the birds chirping made their morning a haven in paradise.

They spent the rest of the day visiting the art galleries, which Sedona was so well known for. Breathtaking creations and hues of wondrous colors provided inspiring scenery. It made her feel as if she was in heaven, with no wish to ever leave. Aimlessly, they wandered all day.

Morning came, and they rented a jeep. Their day of exploration had just begun. Constructed in the thirteenth century were the ruins of Montezuma's Castle. When the United States army scouts came across it, they thought it was built by the Aztec culture and therefore named it after the Aztec ruler. They were amazed with its intricacy. Completely protected, it was intact, nestled high in cliff dwellings. This had been the "Golden Age" of the Sinagua civilization.

They were daring builders as the castle stool five stories high with twenty rooms under overhanging cliffs. Standing for over six hundred years, this was the best preserved prehistoric structure in the Southwest.

The Sinagua were peaceful village dwellers and their communities consisted of many families living together. Daily activities for the women included gathering plants, water from the river below, washing clothes, and cooking, while the men hunted for food, made tools, performed daily rain rituals, and thanked the spirits.

They enjoyed the running water at the banks of Beaver Creek. Birds chirped and dashed through the rows of trees. The afternoon sun created a hallway of light. So harmonious was the setting, it was difficult to leave.

Then, a chilling breeze brushed against Dave's back and the throb of haunting drums echoed in the distance.

"Do you hear the drumming?" he asked.

"I don't hear anything," she replied.

He looked in the direction the drumming came from.

"I know what I heard," he remarked.

Deep in thought, he felt bewildered. The current visitations were starting to get on his nerves. The souls of their ancestors would not allow him peace.

"Let's go to Tuzigoot like we planned, okay?" she interrupted him.

"Okay," he said reluctantly.

It wasn't long before they arrived at Tuzigoot, Apache for "crooked water," one of the largest pueblos built by the Sinagua. The labor constructing the site had to have been backbreaking; its entirety was rock and adobe mortar, massive but poorly balanced. Perched atop a ridge high above Verde River with two stories and one hundred and ten rooms, the community had been occupied from about 1000 A.D. to the 1400's when it was abandoned. There were few exterior doors; the dwellers entered by ladders, from openings in the roofs.

She took his hand as they walked up to the pueblo remains. Examining the exterior and interior they found what was left of many rooms up and down the hills. Still standing was the doorway that led upstairs to the terrace. They stood atop and viewed the countryside and surrounding areas that were used for farming. The mystery engulfed him, as the wind howled such strange noises.

The next day they went hiking at Boynton Canyon, a sacred place. Soon they were enveloped by an euphoria that was magical. Their voices echoed through out the canyons and with all the excitement and energy they started climbing but couldn't stop. By the time the sun was setting, the sting of the winds whipping around their faces were brutal. Surfacing before him were angry spirits.

"Let's go. The spirits do not want us here," he announced.

"How do you know that?" she asked curiously.

"I see spirits pointing for us to get out," he replied.

"What do you mean? What kind of spirits?" she asked.

"Just believe me, okay? I am not losing my mind."

Next day they found themselves mesmerized by Palatki Indian ruins and yet he had a strange feeling that the ancestors were still here. Then something touched his shoulder but when he turned no one was near him. He kept looking around as if soon they would present themselves.

"What's the matter?" asked Desiree.

"Just the spirits playing tricks on me again," he replied.

It was an inspiring place, which they spent all day exploring. Finding ruins intact and rock art visible made him wonder what life had been like back then. He was so excited that he began to walk ahead of her. Then suddenly all alone, Desiree panicked.

An owl shrieked as a solar eclipse fell upon them.

"Where are you?" She yelled out.

"Over here," he called back.

She turned to see him; then in an instant he was gone. She could not believe her eyes. How could he be there one minute and then disappear? She screamed. She cried. She felt such a devastating loss. Her whole world was empty now. She searched the grounds and asked everyone she came across if they had seen him. No one had, so she went to the forest ranger for help.

They searched and searched, and when nothing came up they told her to go home and get some rest. They would continue looking in the morning.

Morning came. She returned to the Palatki Indian ruins, where the forest rangers insisted that she leave. She was only in their way.

Ignoring the advice, she searched on her own. As the sun started to set, she had no choice but to go back to the cabin.

As the days continued, Dave could be found nowhere. Finally, forest rangers told her they could no longer continue. It had been a week since she had last seen him, and they had searched by air, water, and on foot. So she had to let it be, but she was never going to stop looking.

As the days went by she cried uncontrollably. Her world had changed from a state of extreme happiness to one of despair and loneliness, with emptiness beyond belief.

The next day she refused to get out of bed; self-pity had set in. Everywhere she looked she could see Dave's loving face, and she cried again. A prisoner in the rented cabin, she did not want to leave. At least, there she had him near her, even if it was just illusions.

A knock sounded at the door but she ignored it. The knocking grew insistent.

"I know you are in there," demanded a familiar voice.

She opened the door; it was Micki.

"Desiree, you have got to go out and get some air. You can't keep yourself locked up," the woman said.

"I don't want to live anymore," she responded.

"You can't just die. Dave would not want that," replied Micki. "I know someone who can help you. She is a psychic and has helped many detectives find missing people."

"Really?" Hope sprang up in Desiree's heart.

"Yes, she is extremely talented," Micki replied.

"When can I meet her?" she asked.

"I will call her and set up a meeting. I'll let you know."

Next morning Desiree awoke with renewed energy.

"Hi, Micki. What have you got for me today? Any news?"

"Felini says she will meet with you tomorrow at 10 a.m. at her place. Here's her address and phone number, please confirm with her that you will be there."

Desiree arrived early for the meeting.

"Good morning, Felini. How are you?" she asked.

"Just fine, dear. Please have a seat." Felini was a heavy set woman with long black hair, and she wore a lavender, loose fitting dress with embroidery throughout the yoke. Her eyes glowed with warmth and confidence.

"How long have you been helping people?" she asked.

"When I was very young I had visions that terrified me. I thought I was going crazy so I never verbalized them. Until one day. I had awaken to see my vision broadcast on the morning news. I sat in a corner in terror. I trembled and tears overwhelmed me. Then my mother walked in. She had never seen me so emotionally distraught."

"Felini, what did you see?" she urged.

"I tried to gain my composure, then said, 'There is a child buried in that rumble.'"

At that precise moment another news broadcast flashed on the screen, indicating that a child was missing in the horrible tornado that had devastated the city, and they were asking everyone for help.

"Oh my God," my mother said. 'Do you think you can find her?'

"Yes, I think I can," I replied.

"Who is in charge of finding the missing girl?"

"I will get you Sergeant McCalfy," replied the dispatcher.

"Sergeant McCalfy here. How may I help you?"

"I can show you where the child is."

"How?" asked the sergeant.

"I visualized it in a dream."

"You've got to be kidding. Is this a joke?"

"No, Sergeant, this is no joke. I am the only thing you've got. A child's safety depends on it."

"I'll round up my men and pick you up," he replied.

"The sergeant was shocked as I led them right to the child. From there on I was well known for my psychic abilities but the greatest reward was seeing the happiness I had brought to these people. I want you to know I will give it all I've got. We may not come up with anything. There are no guarantees in situations like this," she explained.

"I will never stop looking for Dave. He is my life and I have to do something. Felini, please," she begged.

"Okay, let's start tomorrow. It will have to be exactly where you saw him last," Felini said.

They went to Palatki; the woman wanted to meditate quietly to see what she could pick up. She meditated for a long time before she spoke.

"He's still here. He is also devastated by the separation."

"Where is he? Please tell me," Desiree cried.

"I feel his presence, but I don't know his exact location. We will have to try again in a few days," Felini replied.

"No, let's do it today," she said persistently.

"Desiree, you don't understand. This takes a lot of energy; I need to rest a day or so. Then we will try again," Felini replied.

"Of course, whatever you say," she said.

"Take a day off and try to remember exactly the point and time he disappeared. If there was anything unusual-colors, surroundings, smells-write it down so we can discuss it," Felini said.

The next day dragged on for an eternity as she tried to recall anything out of the ordinary.

Sunrise was now upon them and they were out at Palatki again. This time Felini meditated at the ruins, as Desiree slept. The whole day passed by. When she awoke, Felini indicated she had picked up something else. It seemed as if Dave was confused and didn't know where he was. Everything around him was so foreign, from another place in another time.

"What do you mean?" she asked.

"He is seeing things that have existed hundreds of years ago," Felini said.

"Anything else?" she replied.

"No, we'll have to wait until next time. Hopefully, we can get a clearer picture of his surroundings and do some research to piece events together. By everything I have been picking up from him, I believe he may have slipped into another dimension. Time travel, dear," Felini responded.

"Please, explain?" she asked.

"It is the passage into another lifetime. You both have had many lives together one that he is now reliving. The connection has been intense and has carried itself through many lifes where you have both felt that you couldn't live without each other," replied Felini.

"How is that possible?" Desiree asked.

"It is based on the theory of Karma. That we have many lifetimes to do good and for the progress and purification of the spirit," Felini replied.

Days passed. When Felini finally called her, the woman indicated that she wanted to spend the entire week meditating. She felt that Dave was trying to communicate with her.

"Whatever it takes," Desiree replied.

CHAPTER THREE

For days Dave wandered in a strange place and encountered a tribe of Sinaguas who led him to a cave. A large boulder obscured the entrance and once inside cliff dwellings encompassed the area.

The people bowed as he entered, gazing at him with amazement. The arena seemed to have come alive with spirits of the dead floating in a spiral.

"It is he. It is he; Hotevilla has returned," the elders cried.

"What is going on here?" he asked.

"You have been called here by the great spirits; you are the last living male descendant of our lineage," replied one man. You are here to start a new generation of our people, so you may have any of our daughters of your choice."

"I already have a woman of my own. I will not take any of your daughters; and I am not Hotevilla," he replied.

The man was little, stood no taller than five feet and weighed at most ninety pounds. He wore a long buckskin shirt and long moccasins with a beaded wrap around his waist. His skin was dark and he had straight raven black hair, that fell even with his strong jaw line. Wrinkles crossed his face and his piercing eyes were deeply set. He spoke with authority and was insistent. His callous demeanor depicted his ruthlessness as a leader.

"Who are you?" Dave asked.

" I am the chief of this tribe. My name is Yukiuma."

"You are mistaken. I have no lineage here. I must return. You must show me how to get back," he demanded.

"The spirits will not allow that. You have to fulfill your mission here. We will prove to you that you are a descendant of our people," said Yukiuma.

The tribesmen held torches as Dave was led through narrow passages. Pictographs encompassed the area disclosing important events in the history of their people -- trading, farming, pottery making, cooking and hunting game. Tribesmen in procession carried away cradleboards of their dead infants. At an alarming mortality rate, the plague and spirits hovering over them could not be forgotten. The views of the drought, the destruction of the earth, by volcano eruption was part of their past legacy.

Then they came to a chamber where buckskins were draped on the cave walls and Yukiuma went over and removed one.

"This is not me," he said, astounded. Still the likeness was amazing.

"Before you died you told us you would return to us. Now you are here," Yukiuma declared.

" I am telling you again, that is not me. How many times do I have to tell you? Who is beneath the other buckskin?" he asked.

"It is forbidden for you to see," replied Yukiuma.

He walked forward to uncover it but the tribesmen all moved forward with their spears.

Closely guarded he waited until all slept. Then he searched for a way out. It seemed like he had walked for many miles, looking for any direction that seemed familiar. He remembered Palatki well and was confident that he would somehow find it. As dawn approached and he turned near a stream, again he was encountered by the tribe.

"You cannot leave us, so give up. We will always find you because the spirits are with us," replied Yukiuma.

He fell to his knees. "You will have to kill me, for I will not live without Desiree."

Morning came and he was so distraught. He sneaked out of his quarters and went to the chamber. He managed to undrape the second buckskin. To his astonishment it was Desiree. Draped around her neck was the turquoise necklace he had bought her. He couldn't help but notice its unique authenticity. It looked as if it had been imbedded for hundreds of years. Shaken, he wondered how could this be? Then he sobbed.

He went charging to Yukiuma.

"I want an explanation!"

"What are you talking about?" Yukiuma replied.

"Who is the woman beneath the buckskin?" he asked.

"You were forbidden to see that," Yukiuma replied.

"Well, it's a little late for that, isn't it?" he said.

"She was your squaw and forbidden by our people."

"She is my life now, and I will not live without her."

"When you were our chief, Hotevilla, you were a great hunter. Our land was suffering many changes. The weather and our crops failed one after another. Animals were disappearing because water and food was scarce. But your keen hunting ability always provided food for our tribe. Other tribes were migrating and attacking camps to keep their families from starving. It was during the harvest moon when our camp had been attacked while you and your men were out hunting," said Yukiuma.

Not understanding all that was occurring, not believing in life after death and yet he couldn't deny how the visions kept unfolding before him. He saw himself returning from the hunt to a camp destroyed by smoldering fires, the coppery odor of blood, faceless bodies and splattered blood laying everywhere. He kneeled over a pregnant woman and turned her body over, and as though an arrow had penetrated his heart, Desiree's face materializes before him. The horror overwhelmed him. He lifted her lifeless body, and devastated, he yelled out to the spirits that he would find who had done this.

Through the haze of the smoke, a small figure approached. It is Yukiuma. "Only a few survived," he said.

"No, no," "None of this has happened." Dave muttered. Slipping out of his visions. "I will not believe it." So he dismissed it, thinking the spirits were again trying to trick him.

"So now you have returned and must follow the laws of our people," said Yukiuma.

"I have not returned. I am not your chief," he said.

"Why do you deny this? It is a great honor," replied Yukiuma.

"I am not who you think I am. I will not take any of your daughters. I have a woman of my own. If I create a family it will be with my woman and no one else," he insisted.

"You are still as pigheaded as when you led our people, but you have no choice; it is your duty."

"We'll see," he replied.

As Yukiuma turned, he struck him frantically and they battled. The tribesmen entered the cave wildly beating him. Yukiuma motioned at his men to stop. Bleeding heavily, Dave swore he would not surrender to their demands.

"The spirits do not tolerate disobedience. We will let you die for your defiance," demanded Yukiuma. He signaled to the tribe to tie Dave on the travois and leave his body in the fields. Soon they were out of sight.

He moaned with pain. He was going to die here, because he could not move. He prayed for strength to make his journey and for forgiveness. He had never attacked anyone so violently before.

The cries of vultures filled the air, but he did not see them; there was no hope left.

CHAPTER FOUR

As the wind brutally ripped against the plains, Hotevilla had little time and he rode fiercely as the sun was setting. He had been told his grandfather was ill and he wanted to make it to the camp before dark.

"Good evening, Grandfather. I am here now. Anything you wish will be done. Are you in any pain?" he asked.

"Grandson, I am pleased you are here now, for it is not long that I will meet with the ancients in the sky."

"Grandfather you still have many years left," he replied.

"My dear grandson, my time is near and my wishes are that you take over and protect our tribe. Call a tribal meeting now. I am prepared to speak."

The elders and all tribe council members entered to listen to his Grandfather's words. The old chief asked if anyone would be in disagreement that his grandson be the next chief. Because his father had been killed by a buffalo stampede, Hotevilla was the only surviving grandson. They all cheered. Yes, he would be honored. Then the tribesmen left to let his grandfather rest. Only one of the maidens in the tribe remained to watch over him.

It had been many years before Hotevilla was born, when his grandmother had passed on, to meet the ancients in the sky. He knew his grandfather was anxious to meet with her and his son, whom he loved very much. He now felt, the heavy responsibility and wondered how he would do it without his grandfather. Of course the elders would be there for him, but it was just not going to be the same.

He reminisced on the great times he had with his grandfather. The older man had taught him to be proud of their heritage, to respect nature, how to hunt and he made everything they did fun. As a young brave he admired the great chief who was respected by all.

Even the time he wandered into a cave as child and found a grisly bear. He had trembled as the bear growled. Then Grandfather entered the cave and as the wise warrior threw rocks at the bear to distract it, he ran to safety.

"See you are faster than you thought. Not even the fastest rattlesnake could have caught up with you in that rage of terror." Grandfather grinded.

They had both laughed as they caught their breaths. His arms were strong as he lifted Hotevilla on the back of the horse. His face showed he was proud that his grandson thought quickly in the face of danger.

It was a bright sunny morning. Hotevilla took a deep breath as the winds blew. Birds chirped and children played in the woods. He walked over to

Grandfather's teepee. He wanted to see if there was any improvement.

"Good morning, Grandfather."

"My grandson, it is good to see you," replied Grandfather with a smile. But his eyes declared he was not feeling better.

"Grandfather, I will spend all day looking for buffalo," he said.

He wandered for hours not able to get his grandfather out of his mind. He led his horse down to the stream and got off to sit and think for a while. His thoughts were disturbed when he heard splashing in the water. The scent of lavender filtered in the air. He looked up to find a beautiful maiden, poised on the other side. Her smile was soothing.

"Hello. I am Hotevilla, from the tribe of the North."

" I am White Fawn of the North West."

"What are you doing here? Are you lost?"

"Yes, my horse ran away and I have been walking for days."

"Here, you must be hungry," he said, offering the bit of jerky he had in his pouch.

"Yes, thank you." She smiled with gratitude.

"I will take you to your tribe, if that is okay with you?"

" I am thankful. Yes, please take me to my tribe. They will be worried."

He lifted her on his horse. There was lightning in their touch and they both looked at each other and breathed deeply.

It was many hours by horse, but had only seemed like minutes when they approached her village. Her mother came running as they rode up.

"White Fawn, your father is out searching for you. Where have you been?" the woman asked.

"My horse ran away. It was spooked by a rattlesnake. I wandered for days and got disoriented.

Hotevilla was sitting by a stream deep in thought. I approached him for help," she replied.

"We are grateful to you," replied White Fawn's mother.

"Thank you for being so kind," White Fawn echoed.

" I am happy you are safe with your tribe now," he said.

"Please come tomorrow. My father will want to thank you also," she said.

"Till tomorrow then."

It was a long ride back, but his spirits where lifted by her presence that day.

"Grandfather, how are you?"

" I am doing better today, my grandson," the frail old man replied.

"I met a lost squaw today who heats my heart." Hotevilla smiled. "I will meet with her father tomorrow."

"Sounds like you have finally found one that interests you. That is a good thing, my grandson. I would like to meet her. Before the ancients in the sky come for me."

"Grandfather, please, stop talking like that. You are getting better now."

Morning came. He was happy that his grandfather was looking better and he knew he would be welcome at White Fawn's camp.

"Well, there you are. My father is waiting to meet you. Please follow me," White Fawn replied.

They walked into a large teepee and many of tribe were sitting around the campfire.

"Sit. We are grateful that you were around to help my daughter." The great chief passed the pipe.

Hotevilla nodded, smoked, then passed the pipe around the fire.

She is very independent and I am not happy that she was wandering around those days alone. She is like the wind. She wanders with a great deal of confidence in herself. She must be like her parents."

" Are you not her father?" Hotevilla asked.

" I have raised her like my daughter, but we found her near a stream when she was an infant. Her mother must have hidden her from renegade Indians who ambushed the wagon train. We have come to love her as our own. She does not want to live with the white people. She feels this is her home. She seems to be drawn to the outdoors and rivers. It is with great honor that I give you this stallion. White Fawn has raised this mare well and is happy we can offer it to you," the man said.

" I accept this with great honor also." He nodded.

"Now you have to stay for the celebration. Let us go out and sit with the others." Her father motioned.

Hotevilla was seated next to White Fawn, as they were entertained by dancers, and plenty of food was passed around. White Fawn's face glowed and she wore a beaded necklace and buckskin dress which clung close to her body. He could not take his eyes off of her. She smiled sweetly and he was taken. He tried not to show his weakness at that moment. Everyone in the tribe was drinking and laughing. They were all enjoying the food.

"You are always welcome here, Hotevilla, and our people will always be grateful to you," White Fawn's father said.

"You will always be welcome among our tribe also."

" I will take you to your stallion," White fawn replied. Her hair shone in the moonlight as they walked to the corral. "I am happy to give you this horse. He will produce many fine stallions for your tribe." She looked into his eyes. He was lost in hers.

"Will you come again?"

"Yes, I will come again," he said.

The stallion was a fine horse and it followed as he held on to its reins. The moonlight lit the plains for many miles, but he could not get White Fawn out of his mind. None of the squaws in his village had ever intrigued him as she. She was full of spirit, beautiful and gentle.

Arriving at his camp, he went straight to see Grandfather. He looked well, and was sitting up reminiscing.

"What are you thinking of, Grandfather?" He asked.

"Just remembering your grandmother. I see her now as she was. So beautiful and caring. Always making sure the children were well cared for. She had mystical powers and knew when things would happen, before they did. With her by my side we led our people through many harsh winters and diseases. She had the gift of medicine making and taught everyone in the village how to treat their illness. She was the most precious thing in my life. I will look forward to meeting her again when the ancients come for me."

"Did you know when you met her you would marry her?" He asked.

"Yes, my grandson, I had eyes only for her."

" That's how I feel about White Fawn. Only I feel fire within each time I see her, and when we touch lightning penetrates through my body, and I want her to stay by my side forever."

"My grandson, if these are your feeling for her, do not waste anymore time. We never know how many moons will cross our paths and the spirits advise us to take the each day as our last. If she feels the same about you, marry her."

"Yes, my grandfather, you are very wise. I can see in her eyes that she cares for me. She has asked me to come again. I will go tomorrow."

"Hello, White Fawn, how are you today?"

"Hotevilla, it is wonderful to see you. Let me pack some things so we can go riding out by the stream."

The skies had not been as bright lately as they were that day. She rode as if she was born on that horse. They found a clearing where they stopped and sat along the river bank. Her smile and bright eyes set his heart on fire. He bent over and embraced her. She threw her arms around him and they kissed passionately.

"I have been wanting this since I first saw you," she admitted.

"And I you," he confessed.

They ran into the stream and he gently removed her dress, and kissed her breasts. She ran her fingers in his hair, and their passion for each other made them one.

"I brought lunch let's eat," she said after they were both physically sated.

"Fine I am as hungry as a bear." He grinded.

She giggled and placed the food on a blanket where they gazed at each other as they ate.

"White Fawn, you may think this is too soon, but I have never been in love before this. I want you in my life and cannot see it any other way. Will you be my wife?"

"Yes, Hotevilla, I will. I knew when I first saw you that I wanted to spend the rest of my days with you."

"Fine. I want you to meet my grandfather. He is ill and doesn't have much time left. I also have to ask your father for his blessings."

It was a glorious sunset; a sweet aroma filled the air, they smiled, held hands, then both entered his teepee.

"I have something very important to both of us to ask you."

"Yes, what is it?"

"I would like to marry your daughter, with your blessing. We have talked and she feels the same as I. We do not want to wait. My grandfather is ill and I will be chief of our tribe. I will provide and protect her all the days of my life," he replied.

The chief did not answer right away and they looked at each other with fear. Then her father looked at them and walked out of the teepee.

White Fawn cried. They sat there trying to understand his reaction. Then one hour later, her father, mother and grandmother entered.

"We did not want you to marry so soon, but we see the love between you two is very strong and that is enough for us to welcome you into this tribe. White Fawn, you, your mother and grandmother will prepare for the celebration between both tribes."

"My grandfather will be very pleased," Hotevilla replied.

It was the happiest day of his life and he rushed to the village to give grandfather the news. Maybe he would live long enough to see a grandchild.

"Grandfather, Grandfather, I am happier than I have ever been. White Fawn's father has agreed to our marriage," Hotevilla announced.

"It will also be my happiest day. I have a gift for your bride. It has been handed down from generations. You are to place it around her neck during your wedding ceremony. It will bring love, protection and many healthy children," the old chief said proudly.

"Thank you, Grandfather. It is a beautiful necklace."

Much celebration was going on in the village, once everyone heard of his plans to marry. Nothing pleased him more than seeing the look on his Grandfather's face. It glistened like a full moon over the waters.

He could hardly wait to hold White Fawn in his arms again, much less wait for two long weeks. However, time was needed to pass the word to other tribe members in the distance, who would want to attend.

Time seemed to stand still as he wandered in the fields thinking of how to make a better life for White Fawn. Build a larger teepee and corral for breeding the stallion. His life seemed full now.

Time passed slowly, then the day finally came.

"Grandfather, it is time now. Are you ready?"

"Yes, my grandson."

He mounted so they could go as a group and Grandfather would be more comfortable. In a few hours they were there and White Fawn's father smiled as he greeted everyone.

He took grandfather's arm as they walked to the clearing where the marriage was to take place.

Hotevilla was breathless when he saw White Fawn walking into the arena. She was far more beautiful than the last time he had seen her and she sparkled with excitement.

They stood there while the medicine man gave his blessing. His heart heavy with love, he placed the turquoise necklace on his bride. They kissed and sealed the ceremony.

Together they looked over at his grandfather. His eyes twinkled with delight. He lifted his arms. Everyone yelled and the dancing began.

"Finally we are alone, my love," he whispered to her hours later. He kissed her breasts and rode his hands to her private area. Then he thrust himself inside and felt her heat and wet lips crying for more.

CHAPTER FIVE

As he drifted out of his vision Dave tossed, turned then awakened to find himself tied down. It was cold and dark and he didn't know where he was.

A light flickered in the distance and soon an Indian maiden was by his side. She untied the ropes around his hands and feet and motioned for him to be quiet, as she dragged him to a riverbed where a kiva was hidden behind trees.

"I will return to help you. Stay put," she said.

Again he slipped into another vision. The spirits were active in bringing all this chaos into his life. He saw White Fawn running to the teepee. He entered.

"What is the matter?"

"I heard the women gossiping about me. That because I am white I will bring nothing put pain and devastation to the tribe. They say you should have married a full blood. The mixed blood of our child will only bring weakness they say."

"They are wrong. Our love is strong and we will create a child who will bring many people together. You will see. This is a good thing," he responded. "Now stop those tears. We don't want our child to know sadness." He bent over and gently kissed her cheeks. "My love you will see."

"Yes, you are right, and I love you so," she replied.

Many moons passed. The sky glowed red as it settled against the sun. He ran to his Grandfather's side as the old warrior uttered his final words.

"I am happy to have seen you marry. You are happy with your squaw. Soon you will have a child and this makes me so proud. I may be gone but you will feel my presence. My heart will always be here with you. I have lived a long and happy life. I know I will not make it through this night, for I have had the visions of the ancients. They are preparing for me and I yearn to be with my love. It is a great honor to be lifted by them. So I ask you not to be sad, but to be brave, for we all go when our time has come. I will walk in the forest tonight to meet them."

He grabbed his Grandfather's arm and held the man close to him. As a warrior he tried to hold back the tears.

"I will never forget you, I know you will be well taken care of," he cried.

"My love will never die for you, my grandson."

As a young brave he had been taught that when the ancients called, the chosen had to go alone into the forest to meet them. His heart sank as his frail Grandfather walked into the night.

Many more seasons passed. They were blessed with a son who had the same color of eyes as his great-grandfather as well as a twinkle, which made Hotevilla believe it was the old chief's spirit with them again. They were honored. Many months thereafter White Fawn was again going to have another child. The winter had been very cold and food was scarce.

"My love, we will leave before sunrise to hunt and bring back plenty of food for our tribe," he promised.

They had traveled far and searched all day. It seemed as if every living thing had disappeared. Then in a clearing he saw a buffalo and before long they had her tied up. They shouted with happiness to be able to bring this to the squaws and children. The hunters were anxious to see the look on their faces. The tribe had not had meat in a long time.

All of a sudden, he had a desperate feeling and began riding faster. Then when he reached the top of the hillside, he gasped with horror. The camp had been attacked. He rode faster. As he reached bottom there was nothing left. Bodies lay everywhere. Each warrior searched for his family. Then he saw White Fawn. He ran to her side.

"Who did this," he yelled.

"I love you and we will meet again," she said with her last breath. Then she fell into death.

"No, no," he screamed to the gods. "How could you let this happen? It was not time to take my squaw and my child."

The mountains roared, as the wind rushed through the trees and the storm swept the bodies down the ravine.

Tossing and turning Dave awoke and was astounded by what he had just experienced.

"No, no how can this be" where the only words that came to him.

CHAPTER SIX

Morning Star returned to her village and gathered all the clothing she could find.

"What are you doing and where have you been?" asked Yukiuma.

"Just thought I would give all this to Little Hummingbird. She is without and I have so much," she replied.

"My daughter, you are so good to our people," he said.

When Yukiuma retired, Morning Star snuck out and returned to the strange man she had rescued. His muscles were contracting from the pain, and he was still delirious.

"Desiree, is that you?" he cried out.

"No, I am Morning Star. I have returned to help you."

With a pouch of water, she tilted his head so he could drink, then tore apart the clothing to use as bandages. She patted the wet cloths on his face then washed his wounds and tied clean cloths securely in place to stop the bleeding.

"You will be safe here. I will return tomorrow to check on you," she said.

He was so weak he just nodded. Soon his eyelids where shut and she covered him with a blanket as she left.

Upon arriving everyone was still sleeping and she was relieved that no one had missed her. Her thoughts were on the man she had hidden in the kiva by the river. He was in so much pain and she wanted to stay near him.

It was a busy morning and all the women in camp where doing their daily duties. Slipping away without anyone noticing was easy.

As she entered he was still sleeping and his bandages were heavily soiled with blood. She didn't want to wake him, so she went outside and sat below a large oak tree. The grasslands blew back in forth with a hypnotizing effect. Soon she was asleep.

It was almost dark when she awoke. Rushing around, she removed the bloody bandages and washed him down, trying not to focus on his strong body. She turned but found she was admiring every inch of him. She wanted to make him as comfortable as she could. She wished he were well enough to hold her in his arms and kiss her savagely; this became her consent fantasy.

" I have to leave and will return again tomorrow," she said.

She found it harder and harder to leave him; this man had stepped into her life and he didn't even know she was there.

"Morning Star, where have you been spending all your time," asked Yukiuma.

"Why do you ask, Father?" she replied.

"You haven't been seen around the camp lately," he said.

"It has been so beautiful lately and the spirits have crossed my path, telling me to enjoy all that nature has provided," she said.

"Do not wander far," Yukiuma replied.

For many days she cared for the man before she saw any improvement. Then the next morning as she entered he was sitting on the cot.

"I brought you food. You must be hungry by now," she said. She broke pieces of bread and urged him to eat.

"Why are you helping me?" he asked. He looked at her suspiciously.

"It is wrong to leave someone to die. I don't agree with my father's decision," she replied.

"You are Yukiuma's daughter?" he asked.

"Does that surprise you?" she replied.

"Yes, it does. What will your people think?" he asked.

"They do not know. If they find out I will be in great danger. My father believes that anyone who disobeys the spirits should die. Our life depends on them, for they are the keepers of the earth. Without their blessings we would not survive. Even though I am his daughter the punishment would be more severe for defying him."

"I am thankful for your help and I will leave in the morning. I don't want to risk your life also," he said.

"You are not strong enough yet to journey alone," she replied.

"I have to return to my people. I am feeling much better now," he said. "Why have you not married?"

"The elders are the only male survivors, a plague took the generation of children who died at infancy. Many full moons ago the younger males in our camp went out to hunt but never returned. In anger Yukiuma asked the spirits why. They told him that they would send someone more fit to carry on the blood line of our people. That's why he believed the spirits sent you here. You where the answer to the continued survival of the Sinagua people."

" I wish I could help, but I don't belong here." He paused. "I live in another time. We believe in having one woman for each man. I will not betray her. We have free will to do what we choose to do. No one can make demands or have the right to choose for us. That is our right and freedom. Do you understand?" he said.

"Do I not please you?" she asked.

"You are beautiful and I am thankful, but I cannot stay here," he said.

" I don't understand and how can you deny the survival of our people?" she said.

"I am not the answer. It is not up to me. I have another life that I have to return to. I will not let anyone stop me. Please understand," he replied.

"Then, please let me return with enough food to carry you on your journey," she replied.

"I will only wait till dawn," he said.

With the sting of tears trickling down her cheeks, she left. Upon returning to the camp her father had a suspicious look on his face.

"What is it, Father?"

"The body we left in the fields is gone. Do you know anything of this?"

Her heart sunk and knees trembled. " Maybe wild animals devoured him," she replied.

" There was no trace of footprints," he answered.

"What will you do?" she asked.

"We will dance to the spirits tonight for a vision to locate him and kill him ourselves," he said proudly.

"Great Father, please do not kill him. I am ashamed that I have disobeyed you. I have been tending his wounds. I know I can persuade him, please allow me to do that," she asked.

"You have defied me." Fire bled through his eyes as he looked at her.

"Yes, I have, but in hopes of having many children to carry on the survival of our people. The spirits will be honored with this. Please give him to me," she begged.

"Give me time to ask the spirits," he replied.

"There is no time. He is leaving at dawn," she said.

"Where is he?" he asked.

"I will only tell you if you spare him. The spirits will approve. Have you forgotten that they sent him here for this purpose?" she cried.

"Then lead us to him," he said.

It was a mysteriously cloudy night. The moon was only one quarter of a circle. A green mist filtered through the sky and the winds raged against the trees as if the spirits were whispering to one another. Morning Star led the tribe along the riverbed until they came to the kiva. Then they crawled till they were close to the door, then burst in.

"Tie him up," commanded Yukiuma.

"Morning Star, you have betrayed me," the man yelled, as he looked at her with disgust. "I should have known better."

"I didn't plan to. It is the only way, and you are not strong enough. You will find our ways pleasing," she answered.

"Never, I will never," turbulently he replied.

Morning came and she stepped out to meditate. She asked the spirits to help him adjust to their ways and find peace with himself and to bless them with many children.

After a few hours she returned to the captive, who was guarded by one of the elders.

"You can leave now," she said. She patted his head with a wet cloth.

"Get away from me," he demanded, his face contorted.

She called the elder to watch him, as she stepped out again. The village women were busy washing clothes. She wanted to be alone, so she wandered into the grasslands, where she enjoyed the sounds of nature while gathering plants. She could not get the man's fierce looks out of her mind. She hoped in time he would change.

Many hours later she became excited when she had found a unique blend of plants. She went to see Little Hummingbird who had learned much from her mother, the great medicine woman.

"Help me blend these herbs," she asked.

She later went to draw water and poured the herbs in the pitcher. She was anxious for the man to drink the herbs. They were well known to stimulate sexual desire and he would be in a trance like state.

Evening came and she prepared their meal but he would not eat.

"Please have something," she pleaded.

The fury in his eyes told her he would not forgive her easily.

"If you will not eat then drink this water."

She left it in front of him and stepped outside.

It had been an extremely hot day. He smelled the drink first, took a little sip and waited before he drank more. His thirst could not be satisfied, so he continued till it was all gone.

The next day he entered their quarters to find a growling wolf. The beast's eyes were fierce and he snapped viciously. He looked around for an object to strike him with, then Morning Star entered. At the sight of her, the wolf calmed down and rubbed gently against her. She stared at him and astonishing at it might seem the wolf exited peacefully.

"How did you do that?" asked Dave.

"Our ancient ancestors tell us it is mind power. He is my power animal. He watches over me. I told him with my mind to leave in peace, that I was fine and thanked him for his protection," she replied.

The weeks passed. She had hoped her man would calm down. Then he began to show signs of ease. She was pleased to start seeing improvement in him.

Then when evening came she heard him breathing heavily. She cuddled up next to him. She ran her hands all over his body.

"Desiree, is that you?" he mumbled.

"Yes, my love," Morning Star replied.

He turned over and kissed her passionately.

It was then, that he realized the woman in his arms was not Desiree. Angry, he pushed her away, although he couldn't explain the severe passion that had overwhelmed him. The urge was so great that he got up and went outside. As the elder followed him, he went to the river to bathe. He drank the water from the river and found that it had a different taste, from that of which Morning Star had been preparing for him. Returning to their quarters, he looked at her in rage.

"What have you been treating our drinking water with?" he demanded.

"I do not understand?" she replied.

"The water in the jug does not taste the same as the river water," he said.

"I have added herbs," she said.

"What kind of herbs?" he asked.

"Herbs to make you feel at ease," she replied.

"What else?" he demanded.

"Nothing else," she replied.

The next morning Morning Star went to visit her father the great chief Yukiuma.

"My daughter what is the matter?" he asked.

"Nothing, Father. I just wanted to visit," she said.

"When will he be ready to become our chief?"

"Not yet, Father. He needs more time to get comfortable with our ways. We need to give him more freedom before he can trust us," she replied.

"My daughter, you have made improvement with this man, and I am pleased. Go now," he said.

Morning Star led him and they sat under a tree.

"We are simple people, our elders farm and make tools," she explained. Every full moon they go into the high mountains and stay overnight. They pray for supernatural powers to fight our enemies. Some have prophetic dreams while others receive visions from the great spirits. They tell us how to better serve our creator and that we must follow the ancient ways.

When we hunt, we do not hunt just to kill. The spirits have taught us to respect all things, animals and the earth. They are sacred to us. We give back what we take. We only hunt when there is need to feed our people, and the spirits bless us with abundance when we obey their commands. The women wash, cook, and gather plants, wood, and watch over our village. We follow the pattern of life our creator has set forth. We live in harmony with the universe. These are our ways and existence," she said.

"Are the women the only ones to watch over the village during the full moon?" he asked.

"Many men are left to guard our camp," she replied.

"When will I be allowed more freedom?" he asked.

"When we prove to my father that you have earned his respect," she said.

"How will we do that?" he asked.

"We will work on it together and by joining him when he has his meals. He will see that you will make a good husband," she said.

" I have not agreed to that," he said.

"Do I not please you?" she asked.

"I need time," he replied.

It all came to Dave now. He realized the water she gave him in the evenings gave him savage sexual desires. It was as if a strange presence had inhabited his body; he didn't know how long he could resist her.

He pretended to drink the water she brought but as soon as she turned he spit it out. It took many weeks before he was feeling like himself again and knew he had to find his way out.

"Are you unhappy with me? You have not touched me in weeks," she asked.

"I have had much on my mind," he answered.

"What is worrying you?" she asked.

"It doesn't concern you," he replied.

He was avoiding answering and she knew why. He was missing his Desiree, he cried out for her in his sleep.

Next day, she went to Little Hummingbird.

"He is losing his desire for me. Do you know of stronger herbs?" she asked.

"I do not know of any other, but I will ask my mother when she returns," her friend replied.

"Let's go and gather all the herbs we can find."

They spent the whole afternoon gathering and talking. Enjoying the fresh air and looking into the crayola blue sky, which presented the largest white cottony clouds, they had ever seen.

The next evening as Dave slept he was awaken by Morning Star's kisses and roving hands. In anger he hit her violently with his fist. Outside the elder heard her crying and burst into their quarters.

"Your father will find out about this," he said.

Moments later Yukiuma came charging into their quarters with many men.

"Tie him up," the chief commanded.

"Father, please, what will you do?" cried Morning Star.

"It is not up to you anymore. He has shown no respect for our people or you," replied Yukima.

Morning came and the tribesmen hurried as they tied him up against a pole, placing logs, brush and stone around the pedestal.

"No," begged Morning Star.

Lighting the brush, they all chanted. Fire had engulfed him. Then out of nowhere a black cloud engulfed the sky, as if something was coming to annihilate all of them. Trees were tossed and uprooted by the approaching whirlwinds which blew through the camp causing everyone to run. Thunder surrounded them as lightning stuck their quarters, setting everything on fire.

"Release him now, or you will all die," demanded the gods. "It is not time for him to die. You will keep him guarded until I tell you so," insisted the ancient spirits.

They did as the gods demanded but Yukiuma was very bitter towards this outsider. He didn't understand why the gods were sparing him. If they defied the gods there would be no hesitation.

Everyone rushed around putting out the fires and tending their quarters. It took many days of hard work to cleanup the damage. Yukiuma was pleased with their progress. They knew the gods would remove their hearts if they displeased them again. That fury had been prophesized in the great tablets.

Morning Star tended his burns and Dave recognized her unconditional love. For the first time he saw all her good qualities. She loved all things and cared for anything that became injured. She had a healing power not like any other and she was always called upon to heal others. She had a special light within that brought joy to others. She was a small, thin woman with long black hair, clear sparkling hazel eyes and a dazzling smile. She wore a multiple-strand bead necklace, moccasins and buckskin dress. She deserved a good man. She was a good woman and he felt guilty some how that he could not return her love.

He could not get Desiree out of his mind or heart. He didn't know how long he had been gone but he heard her spirit calling out to him, and as if she could hear him, he cried out.

"I will be with you soon, my love."

He wondered how this could be. It was Desiree's voice. He knew it must be their strong connection to each other, from the beginning something drew them together that was eerie. He knew now he had to plan an escape.

Days passed and Dave was heavily guarded. He asked Morning Star to gather wild nuts so they could have them with their next meal. She went happily. Having him near her was all she wanted. She was beginning to accept his strong devotion to Desiree, knowing he would never love her. But she felt privileged to have him by her side.

It was a beautiful sunny day, as the winds blew against the grasslands it created a velvety sheen across the land and the birds sang joyfully. Morning Star loved being outdoors and she spent all day enjoying the fresh air and sunshine. She had gathered wild grapes, nuts, acorns, sunflower seeds, walnuts and wild potatoes. She was excited with all she had found today and eager to prepare the evening meal.

Upon arriving back, she found her man no longer there. Neither were any of the elders. She went to ask the other women. They replied that there was much excitement in the camp. It had been many years since they had seen a buffalo and they rushed around painting each other's faces. They prepared cattail pollen, incense and danced to the spirits asking them to help them capture the buffalo. Gathering their wolf skins, traps, clubs, and arrows they fled to find it.

"Did they take the man?" she asked.

"I do not know," replied the older woman.

Later that evening the men returned with the buffalo. Morning Star rushed to her father.

"Where is the man called Dave? Did you take him?" she asked.

"What do you mean?" he said.

"When I returned, he was not in our quarters," she said.

"He can't go far. But first, we must celebrate. Our people have not had buffalo meat in a long time. In the morning I will gather the others and ask the spirits for their help," he said.

In the moonlight, everyone participated in the ceremonial dances around the campfire, while the wolves howled. They thanked the spirits for bringing the buffalo to their camp and giving them the strength to capture it.

Dave felt renewed. His escape was successful. He was free and had more energy and zest for life than he had had in a long time. He walked with greater hope that he would this time accomplish his journey. There was a silence for days and this made him very uneasy. He didn't hear anything, not nature, not wind. This was not natural and he wondered somehow they might be watching him. He couldn't worry about that now. He had to focus on getting out alive. His food and water was gone and the wilderness had no signs of animals or vegetation. Soon he was delirious and losing his bearings.

"Desiree, where are you?" he cried out, "I cannot live without you!" Nothing looked familiar and he could not go on any longer. His strength was failing. He would soon die.

The next morning he awoke in great despair to see that everything around him was a blur. He heard chanting in the background and feared Yukiuma's men were closing in on him and he would be captured again.

"I have no life like this," he moaned, lifting the lance and pointing it at his heart.

"Dave, Dave, wait!" cried a voice in the distance.

He turned but could not see anything. The scream was closer now and he listened again, but decided it was a trick, so he lifted the lance again.

"Please, please, Dave, don't do it. I cannot live without you," yelled Desiree.

Then he felt Desiree's lips against his, and they embraced in each other's arms. They both cried.

Colors never seen before encompassed the sky.

The spirits looked down on both of them and decided to let go. The sacrifice Dave was willing to make insured them that no one could ever rule over his love.

Then like fireflies into the night they disappeared whispering to each other. "We will find someone else."

THE END

About the Author

As a child it was difficult for me to stay indoors. I loved the feeling of fresh air on my face and enjoyed watching the animals in my surroundings. Especially the birds and squirrels, their look, so precious, always caught my eye.

As I grew and was able to drive. I spent all my time exploring side roads, lakes, mountains and oceans. The more I saw the more I wanted to see and to this day I still explore the wonders of this world.

In my later years I found fascination with spirituality, ancient cultures, and nature. I realized my creativity emerging. I wrote from the heart and started with poetry. Analyzing life and conditions. I found my true passion in writing. Past Becomes Present is my first novel, email me at www.pbp777@aol.com .

www.ingramcontent.com/pod-product-compliance
Ingram Content Group UK Ltd.
Pitfield, Milton Keynes, MK11 3LW, UK
UKHW040016200726
13854UKWH00001B/239